This Winnie-the-Pooh
book belongs to

. . . .

First published in Great Britain 2020 by Farshore
This edition published 2022 by Farshore
An imprint of HarperCollins*Publishers*
1 London Bridge Street, London SE1 9GF
www.farshore.co.uk

HarperCollins*Publishers*
1st Floor, Watermarque Building, Ringsend Road
Dublin 4, Ireland

Illustrations by Eleanor Taylor and Mikki Butterley

ISBN 978 0 0085 1397 9
Printed in Great Britain by Bell and Bain Ltd, Glasgow
001

MIX
Paper from
responsible sources
FSC™ C007454

FSC
www.fsc.org

Winnie-the-Pooh

A Song for Christmas

Farshore

As soon as Pooh woke up on Christmas Eve and pressed his nose against the frosty glass, he knew that it was going to be a **humming** sort of day.

Snow was piled up against the windows and against his door. With a **heave** and a **ho** he pushed the door open and padded out into the snowy forest.

He went to call on his good friend, Piglet, who was very excited indeed to go on a snowy, **hummy** adventure.

But they hadn't gone very far when ... with an **"Ohh!"** ...

Piglet completely disappeared.

Pooh looked left and Pooh looked right.

"Piglet must have gone home," he sighed
to himself.

"Pooh, help!" came the muffled voice
of Piglet, somewhere near his toes.

Once Piglet had been **pulled** out of the hole and had **shaken** the snow from his ears, they **climbed** up to a safer place.

"How does the hum go?" asked Piglet.

"Well it doesn't really go yet," explained Pooh. "It starts and then stops before it's got to the **hummy** part. It's more of a song," he continued, wisely, "but with no tune."

"Oh, I see," said Piglet, who didn't.

But as they sat there with the wind **whipping** around them, the **hum** that had become a **song** did start to go and it went something like this:

"Oh the **snow** is very **snowy**,

And the **wind** is very **blowy**,

And **Bear** is very **knowy**

That his **tummy** has a **rumble**,

And that rumble in his **tumble**,

Can only mean **one** thing

And so we **sing**...

and sing...

and **sing**..."

"But why are we singing?" interrupted Piglet.

"For the **rumble**," replied Pooh. "Haven't you ever heard of **singing for your supper?** Come along."

Piglet wasn't sure he had, but it was rather **cold** for a Very Small Animal so he happily followed Pooh into the **warm** to practise the hummy song.

Together they sang the song with

Pooh singing **high** and Piglet singing **low** and then with

Pooh singing low and Piglet singing high.

"And now it's time to call on our friends and sing for them. Maybe they'll even have a little smackerel of something," Pooh announced.

First they called on Kanga, Roo and **bouncy** Tigger. There wasn't any food for them to eat, but they **sang** their song anyway.

Roo wanted to join in.

"You and Tigger can **bang things,**" said Pooh, and so they did.

Much to **Pooh's disappointment** there wasn't any food at Rabbit's either, and what with Tigger's **bouncing** and all the **banging**, the **song** didn't go very well at all.

"This will never do," announced Rabbit. **"What you need is order."**

And with that, he lined the animals up with the larger ones at the back and the smaller ones at the front.

"**Much better,**" he said, and he marched them all to Owl's tree.

"Who's there?" asked Owl.

"Us," said Pooh. "And we're hungry," he added.

"Well it can't be 'us'," said Owl, "because I'm here, finishing the last bite of my supper."

But Owl was kind enough to lend them candles to light their way and he agreed to join them as they went to call on Eeyore.

Eeyore was in his usual **gloomy place** and, as they began their song, he let out a **long, low, sorrowful moan.**

"**Oooohhhhh**, rumbles indeed, you don't need to tell me about those," he groaned. "With all this snow, I haven't had a **bite** to eat since Tuesday ... or was it Thursday — they're all the same to me."

This reminded everyone just **how hungry** in the **tummy** and cold in the toes they were.

But Pooh knew just the place to go ...

Everyone sang as they walked and, hearing them coming, Christopher Robin already had his door open when they arrived.

"Come in!" he called. "There's a **warm fire** and **plenty to eat.**"

And so there was ... There was one **big** cake, lots of little cakes and **tasty** spiced pies.

Once they had all eaten **more than was sensible,** they settled around the fire and sang the song again for good luck.

Accompanied by Roo's **banging** and
Eeyore's low **melodic moans**, it really
was the **perfect song** for Christmas.

"I was right about it being a **humming**
sort of day," yawned Pooh that night,
as he tucked himself into his cosy bed.
"But hums are tricky things and they
often need **good friends** to make
them **just right.** Honey helps too,"
he added thoughtfully and that night
his dreams were full of it!

Enjoy other wintery tales with Winnie-the-Pooh and friends!

A Tree for Christmas
ISBN 9781405291101

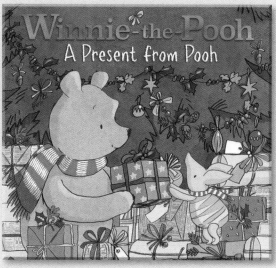

A Present from Pooh
ISBN 9780755501229

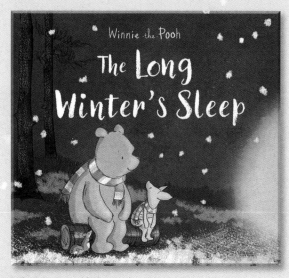

The Long Winter's Sleep
ISBN 9781405294591

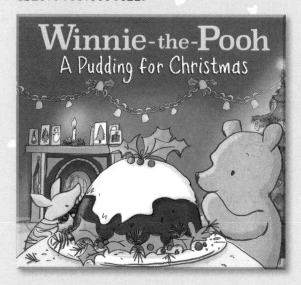

A Pudding for Christmas
ISBN 9781405297875